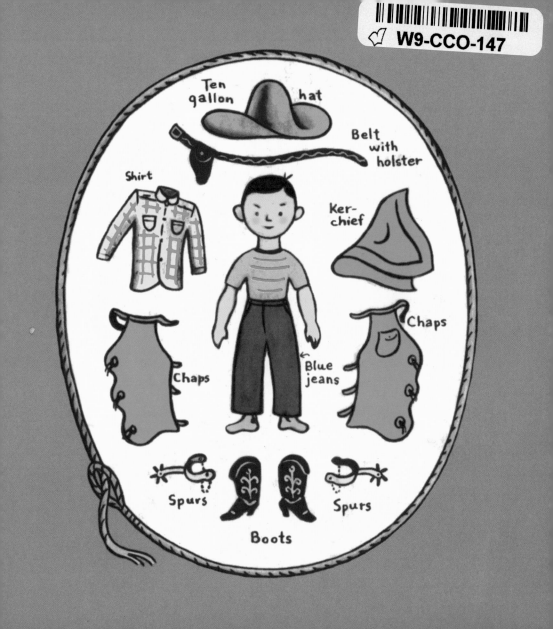

bedroll—blankets rolled up

bit—a metal bar in a horse's mouth

brand—a mark or sign that indicates ownership

bridle—straps around a horse's head, with bit and reins

bronco—a wild horse, not used to a rider

bucking—kicking by a horse, with head between front legs

bunk—a bed

bunkhouse—a house for cowboys' beds

chaps—leather overalls, open at the back, worn over trousers

chuck wagon—a wagon that carries food and bedrolls for cowboys

corral—a fenced-in yard for cows or horses

curries—brushes a horse's hide with a currycomb

dismounts—gets down from

giddyup—a command to get a horse to speed up

girth—a strap around the body of a horse to hold the saddle in place

mounts—gets up on

ranch—a large farm with grass for cows

range—an open place where cows eat grass

reins—straps used to steer a horse

saddle—a seat for a rider, made of leather

stirrup—the loop at the end of a strap hung from the saddle,
        to hold the foot of the rider

Cowboy Small

Copyright © 1949 by Lois Lenski. Copyright renewed 1977 by Steven Covey and Paul A. Covey.
All rights reserved under International and Pan-American Copyright Conventions. Published in
the United States by Random House, Inc., New York, and simultaneously in Canada by Random
House of Canada Limited, Toronto. Originally published by Henry Z. Walck, Inc., in 1949.
www.randomhouse.com/kids
ISBN 0-375-81075-7 (trade) — ISBN 0-375-91075-1 (lib. bdg.)
Library of Congress Control Number: 00-105720
Printed in the United States of America   November 2001   10 9 8 7 6 5 4 3 2 1
First Random House Edition
RANDOM HOUSE and colophon are registered trademarks of Random House, Inc.

Cowboy Small

Lois Lenski

Random House  New York

"Hi, there!"
calls
Cowboy Small.

Cowboy Small
has a horse.
His name is Cactus.
He keeps him in the barn
at Bar S Ranch.

Cowboy Small
takes good care
of Cactus.
He brushes and curries him.

He feeds him
oats and hay.

He gives him water
to drink.

Cowboy Small
puts the saddle on.
He pulls the girth tight.

"Whoa, Cactus!"

Cowboy Small
puts his left foot
in the stirrup
and mounts.

"Giddyup, Cactus!"

Cowboy Small rides out
on the range.
Cloppety, cloppety, clop!

"Whoa, Cactus!"

Cowboy Small
dismounts.
He fixes the fence.

Cowboy Small makes camp
for the night.
He cooks supper and eats it.
Oh, how good it tastes!

Cowboy Small rolls up
in his bedroll.
He goes to sleep
under the stars.

Next morning,
Cowboy Small rides in the Bar S roundup.

The cowboys round up all the cows.
"Yip-pee! Yip-pee! Yip-pee!"

"Come and get it!"
calls the cook at noon.

Cowboy Small
eats at the chuck wagon
with the cowboys.
They have beef,
red beans, and coffee.

"Yip-pee!
Ride 'em, cowboy!"

Cowboy Small
ropes a calf
in the corral.

Cowboy Small helps
with the branding.
The calves are marked
with the Bar S brand:

$$\overline{S}$$

Cowboy Small
turns the cows back
on the range.

At night,
Cowboy Small
plays his guitar
and sings:

*"Home . . .
        home on the range . . ."*

He goes to sleep
in the bunkhouse.

Next day,
Cowboy Small
rides a bucking bronco.

"Yip-pee!—Yip-pee!
Ride 'em, cowboy!"

Ker-plop!

Cowboy Small
hits
the
dust!

But—
he's a pretty good cowboy
after all!
Cactus is waiting,
so—

"Giddyup, Cactus!"

**Cowboy Small
rides
again!**

And
that's all

about
Cowboy Small!

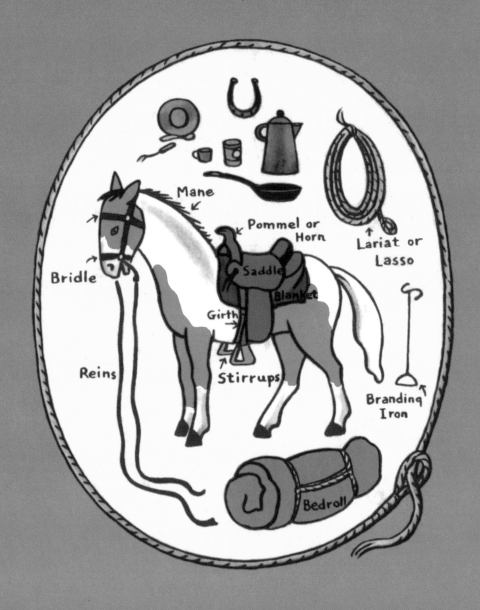